The Galaxy Diner

by Susan Nastasic

Cover Illustration: Laura J. Bryant
Inside Illustration: Laura J. Bryant

About the Author

Susan Nastasic was born and raised in Florida. She received a bachelor of arts degree in studio arts in Greenville, South Carolina. Ms. Nastasic has held a variety of jobs including actress, film producer, teacher, and art director. These jobs have moved her around the United States from New York to Georgia to North Carolina.

Ms. Nastasic enjoys singing country music, painting wall murals and furniture, and running with her dog, Shadow. She was recently married and will spend the next year touring with her husband's musical group.

Text © 2001 by Perfection Learning® Corporation.

All rights reserved. No part of this book may be used or reproduced in any manner whatsoever without written permission from the publisher. Printed in the United States of America. For information, contact

Perfection Learning® Corporation

1000 North Second Avenue, P.O. Box 500

Logan, Iowa 51546-0500

Phone: 1-800-831-4190 • Fax: 1-800-543-2745

PB ISBN-10: 0-7891-5327-0 ISBN-13: 978-0-7891-5327-2

RLB ISBN-10: 0-7807-9716-7 ISBN-13: 978-0-7807-9716-1

11 12 13 PP 18 17 16

Printed in the U.S.A.

Table of Contents

1

Customer Watching

There they go again. Those three little old guys in the corner booth are laughing and giggling like they can't stop. You would think they had just seen the funniest thing on Earth.

But it's just a newspaper. The main story talks about some alien sighting. I don't know exactly. I didn't bother to read it.

THE GALAXY DINER

Around here, folks are always seeing something strange in the sky or landing in a back pasture somewhere. It never turns out to be much. It is usually neon gases or meteorites or something.

My neighbor claimed there were little aliens invading her attic. She was going to be on a talk show in New York.

But she never went. It turned out it was just a bunch of noisy squirrels. So much for space invaders!

Anyway, those three little old guys in the corner booth get a real hoot about any type of alien stories. They always scan the papers. Then they giggle over what they find.

They come into the diner every day except Monday. I've gotten to know them pretty well.

I'm Grace. I help out at the Galaxy Diner. We're the place that's shaped like a flying saucer. That's because we're only about 35 miles away from NASA. That's the place in Florida where they shoot all the rockets up into space.

The whole space theme is pretty played out around here. But the Galaxy Diner is still popular.

The diner looks like a real spaceship. It has a round, silver-domed top. There are small windows circling the roof. Sparkling silver lights light up the entrance.

Working in a flying saucer-shaped diner is embarrassing sometimes. I try not to talk about it at school. But everyone knows anyway. The bus lets me off at the diner every day during the school year.

Even the food has space themes. We serve heavenly hamburgers, out-of-this-world onion rings, and starburst sodas. When someone orders a plutonium pizza or a Milky Way milk shake, I just want to run and hide.

The servers have to dress up like astronauts from outer space. They wear shimmering gold jumpsuits. Even their tennis shoes are gold.

Uncle Roger says it helps create atmosphere. I think they look ridiculous.

Luckily, I don't have to wear the space costume. I just wear a T-shirt that has *GALAXY DINER* printed on it.

My job is to hand out menus and make sure everybody has enough coffee and water. It's a pretty good job for a 12-year-old. Of course, I only got the job because my Uncle Roger owns the place.

My cousin Rudy works at the diner with me. He wears a Galaxy Diner T-shirt too.

Rudy's job is to sweep the floor and help clear away dirty plates. It isn't as good as my job. But he's only ten.

It's not like we get paid all that much or anything. But it is more than a normal allowance.

Plus, we get free candy. There are Jupiter jawbreakers, Rings-of-Saturn Lifesavers, and Moon pops in jars on the lunch counter.

Rudy is really shy. But he's really smart too. I like having him around.

Together, we have fun watching the customers. It's great to have someone to laugh with.

If you really watch people, almost everybody is strange in some way—especially with their food. Take Mr. Longo, for example. He's the manager of the copy store down the street.

He comes in every day on his break. All he orders is a cup of black coffee. Then he just sits there. He stares straight ahead at nothing for exactly seven minutes.

Finally, he takes a sip of his coffee. And he makes a really ugly face. Then he yells loudly, "Hey, Grace, my coffee's cold!"

It used to make me crazy. But Rudy convinced me to just have another cup ready and forget it. Some things aren't worth getting mad over.

Then there's Miss Stella. She's very polite and dainty. You don't expect this because she's kind of heavy. Okay, she's really heavy. The kind of heavy where the fat bulges over her shoes and then again over her knee-highs.

Anyway, after every few bites, she has this weird habit. She daintily holds her napkin up to her face and burps. It isn't a big burp—just a little burp. The funniest little burp you ever heard—like a baby-bird burp.

She always peeps out over her napkin to see if anyone has noticed. Rudy is really good at pretending not to notice. But I have to turn and face the coffeemaker. I can't help giggling.

Speaking of giggling, those three little old guys back in the corner booth have the screechiest laughs you've ever heard. And talk about strange! It's not that they act any weirder than anybody else. But they give off a funny feeling.

Even Rudy's cat, Quasar, knows it. She likes almost everyone. Her favorite thing is to rub up against customers' legs. Sometimes she scares them!

But Quasar took one look at those three old guys and her back arched higher than the Sunshine Skyway Bridge. That's the bridge across Tampa Bay in Florida.

Quasar has a hissing fit whenever they come in. Now we have to put her in the back room when they're here.

That's the kind of weird they are. There's just something strange about them.

They look weird too. Their heads seem a little too big for their bodies. And they always wear striped shirts.

Now that isn't so strange in itself. Almost everybody in Florida wears striped shirts. You don't notice all the stripes until you come back after going on vacation somewhere else.

But I never see these three wear anything else. One guy wears green stripes. One wears blue stripes. And the other one wears red stripes.

Sure, they're colorful. But they look a little goofy—even for old guys.

Their hair is a real sight too! It's gray—like most of the old folks around here. But it has a bluish purple color to it. And it sort of glows. So there's a purple halo around their heads.

These guys really need to switch hairdressers in a hurry. Their heads leave a serious purple stain on the back of our vinyl seat covers. Not even three sprays of cleaning solution and lots of rubbing would get the stains out.

That's why we always seat them in the same booth. That way they don't stain any other seats. And they seem to like it there by the window.

Anyway, right from the start, Rudy and I knew those three were worth watching. And were we right! Just wait 'til you hear what happened after work last Saturday.

We didn't tell anyone because we promised not to. And because Rudy didn't want to do a talk show.

Most people probably won't believe us. But I decided to write it down, anyway. Then, in 100 years or so, when all the planets are friends, somebody may read this and find it interesting.

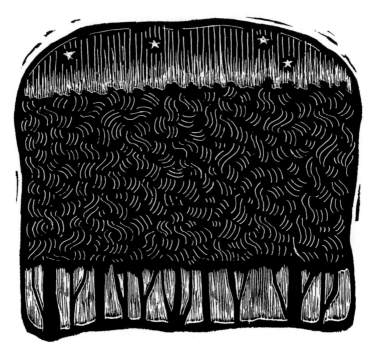

2

The Disappearance

Saturday was a really slow lunch. The county fair was going on across town. Everybody was over there stuffing themselves on cotton candy and those greasy foot-long corn dogs.

Anyhow, we weren't very busy. So Uncle Roger told us to go have some fun.

We thought about going over to the fairgrounds. But we'd already been there three times that week. Just thinking about those corn dogs was reason enough not to go over there again.

It was so hot out! We were in the shade of the famous Galaxy Diner billboard. But I could still feel the sweat rolling down my back. I read the words on the billboard for the millionth time.

We were trying to decide what to do. Suddenly, the three old guys came out of the diner. We must have been really bored to do what we did next. We followed them.

They were on those big three-wheeler bikes. They had big baskets and squeaky horns.

Rudy and I were on foot. But it was still easy to follow them. They were pretty clumsy. And they rode pretty slow.

There were also a lot of stop signs along the way. Whenever they stopped, we caught up with them.

It was easy to follow someone if you watched enough spy movies. The three old guys never had a clue we were there.

Well, they rode right into the trailer park. That wasn't unusual because that was where most of the old folks around here lived. It was a friendly place.

Everybody hung up strings of lights even though it wasn't Christmas. My favorites were the hot-chili-pepper and cactus lights. Rudy liked the cat faces because they reminded him of Quasar.

You could tell what kind of people lived in the trailer by what kind of lights they strung up. We wanted to see what kind of light strings the three old guys had.

But they didn't stop at any trailer. They just kept riding. They rode all the way to the back of the trailer park.

An overgrown hedge grew at the edge of the park. The scary woods were right behind the hedge. The old guys rode right into the middle of all the bushes and vanished!

I looked at Rudy to see if I had imagined it. But I could tell he'd seen the same thing. We knew right then that we were onto something. This was too weird!

We ran over to the spot where they had disappeared. At first we didn't see anything. But then we noticed the thick vines. They were hanging in front of a dark opening in the bushes.

I took a deep breath. The thick hedge was the only thing that separated the trailer park from the scary woods. I really wanted to follow the three old guys. But I really didn't want to go into the scary woods.

Rudy was breathing pretty hard too. We'd never been in the scary woods. Sure we'd been in plenty of woods. We'd even built a tree fort in the woods once near the diner.

But these woods were different. Strange lights and eerie noises came from these woods. And we had heard stories of kids disappearing and never coming back. I knew they were just stories. But why take a risk?

Rudy and I debated. On the one hand, if we didn't go in, we would never know what was up with the three old guys. On the other hand, if we did go in . . .

We decided to draw sticks. The short stick meant we'd go in. The long stick meant we'd go home.

I held the sticks and my breath while Rudy pulled. Of course he pulled the short stick.

Before we could think about it, we held hands and counted to three. Then we tore through the dark vines. We raced past the thick hedge and into the scary woods as fast as we could.

3

The Scary Woods

The scary woods were the coolest woods I'd
ever been in. The trees were really thick. Even the
sun could barely get through. The palm trees
made a roof of palm fronds way up over our
heads.

The ground was covered with tons of brown
leaves. You could jump right in them—if you
weren't too scared. Who could know what might
be underneath?

There was a path of brown leaves right in front of us. We'd come this far. So we had no choice but to follow it.

The woods kept getting darker and darker. Rudy held my hand so tightly it hurt. But I didn't mind. I held his just as hard.

We started running a little. We thought it would be easy to catch up with the three little old guys.

But they must've gotten a sudden burst of energy. Because they were nowhere in sight. We didn't even see their tire tracks in the leaves.

We ran on and on down the path. I thought it would never end.

The trees kept getting closer and closer together. Soon it was totally dark. We couldn't see the sky at all.

The tree branches dipped low. The path seemed more like a tunnel. I wondered if those stories of disappearing kids might be true after all.

I was sweating a lot. I couldn't have let go of Rudy's hand even if I'd tried. Sweat had stuck our hands together.

We were just about to turn back and head home. Suddenly, the path took a sharp turn. We followed it around the corner.

A small, grassy clearing was up ahead. We couldn't believe our eyes. There sat a *spaceship* in the middle of the scary woods!

Of course, we knew what a spaceship looked like. It looked just like the Galaxy Diner.

It had the same silver dome and little round windows all the way around. There was a pink glow around the base of the ship.

Lights were flashing everywhere—white lights and red lights, blue lights and purple lights. There was a really high whistling sound in the air. And it was getting louder by the minute.

We saw a round opening about two feet wide on the side of the spaceship. I figured that was how the three old guys had gotten on board.

Without thinking, I ran right into the opening. I dragged Rudy in behind me. I had never seen Rudy's eyes so big.

A panel slid closed behind us. We were trapped in a real spaceship. We heard a loud whistling. Then the spaceship lifted off the ground.

I started to wish we'd gone to the fair. Then we wouldn't be stuck on this real flying saucer.

We couldn't see anything inside the saucer. It was too dark. But we sure felt it.

Soon I felt like we *had* gone to the fair. And we were riding the fastest ride. The spaceship spun and shook wildly. Rudy and I were pressed flat against the side. We couldn't have moved if we'd wanted to.

We must have both passed out then. Because the next thing I knew, the spaceship had stopped spinning. But my head hadn't.

I felt like I'd just gotten off the backwards Twirl-a-Gig. It's a good thing I didn't eat a corn dog beforehand. Rudy didn't look so good either.

Right then the panel slid open. We didn't know what to do. But we figured we'd better get out of the spaceship quickly.

We jumped down onto soft ground. We looked around quickly and started running. We hid behind the first thing that caught our eye. It was a huge sign that flashed these words.

We'd never heard of the Terra Grill. And we didn't know where Planet Zora was. But it sure wasn't in the scary woods!

4

Planet Zora

Rudy and I took a moment to look around. We could tell we were really far away from home.

Planet Zora was one strange place!

It seemed like night because the sky was black. But there were lights everywhere. Even the ground sparkled with lights.

Little puffs of dust moved beneath our feet. The puffs were filled with gold sparkles of light. Soon our shoes were covered in gold dust.

Everything had tiny light specks running through it. The sign we hid behind looked like some kind of metal. The tiny lights moved all through it. They looked like they were swimming inside the sign.

It was like a big jar of gold glitter had spilled over the whole planet. Only the glitter wasn't just stuck on. It moved inside everything.

All of the buildings were made of the same glittery lit-up metal. Only they weren't shaped like our buildings. They were shaped like lamp shades! They looked like tall, lopsided lamp shades stacked on top of one another.

There was a thin pole between each lamp-shade shape. Some were stacked as many as five high. That was probably as high as a 30-story building.

It was beautiful in that futuristic sort of way. If anybody in Florida ever saw it, they'd probably try to turn it into an amusement park—or at least make it into condos.

I didn't understand how anybody could sleep in those buildings. They were so bright. Maybe the people on this planet didn't sleep.

There were tons of people everywhere. They weren't Earthlings. But they sort of looked like us. I decided to call them *Zorians* since we were on Planet Zora.

So anyway, all these Zorians were running around. And I mean *running*. They were moving really fast. We heard them laughing and talking as they zoomed by.

I tried to see what color their skin was. Everybody always drew aliens with green skin. I wanted to see if this was true. But I couldn't tell because they were so covered in glitter dust.

Their clothes were covered with dust too—and filled with those little lights. I'd never seen anything like it before. They definitely didn't shop at the mall!

It looked like they wrapped themselves in lots of see-through scarves. So many that they weren't see-through anymore.

The fastest Zorians flew past us. With their lighted gold skin and clothes, all we saw was a flash of light—and a hat. The hat thing really didn't fit in. It was so strange.

They weren't wearing weird hats. They weren't wearing gold lit-up hats either.

They were wearing baseball hats, sun hats, and cowboy hats. One even had on a Pilgrim hat. In other words, they were wearing Earth hats!

THE GALAXY DINER

We didn't want to stand out too much. We didn't know how Zorians felt about Earthlings. So we covered ourselves in glittery gold dust. We even smeared it on our faces.

Rudy took his baseball hat out of his back pocket. He made me wear it.

I found a cowboy hat on the ground. Some Zorian had lost it as he sped by. I stuck the hat on Rudy's head.

It was way too big for him. It kept falling over his eyes. But it was still a pretty good disguise.

With our hats and glitter dust, we didn't look too much like Earthlings—unless you looked really close. We weren't sure what would happen next. But we were ready.

Everything was so new and different. We hadn't paid any attention to where the spaceship had gone. We knew we had to find the three old guys from the corner booth. They were our only hope of ever getting home again.

Rudy was scared they'd be mad at us for sneaking aboard their spaceship. I was just hoping we could find them!

But we didn't see the spaceship anywhere. And we couldn't find the three old guys, either.

Rudy looked upset. I thought he might start to cry. But he didn't.

I kind of felt like crying too. But I didn't want Rudy to feel worse. Now I understood why my dad always told me never to go home with strangers.

5

The Terra Grill

We started walking. But it wasn't really like walking. It was like high-speed floating.

Every step we took was like a giant leap. We could run really fast. It was so much fun!

Rudy said it was because Planet Zora had less gravity than Earth. I didn't care why. I just wanted to race.

No wonder everybody had been flashing by us. We felt like we were flying. Rudy's cowboy hat kept falling off. Finally, we tied it on with some string he had in his pocket.

We had another problem besides the hat. We didn't know where to go. And we were covering a lot of ground in a short time.

It was one thing to go slow to nowhere. But to go there really fast was a little scary.

So we stopped worrying about where we should go. Instead we started racing each other. We tied almost every time.

Rudy won twice. Even on Earth, he's really fast for a ten-year-old. But on Planet Zora, he was superfast.

After a while, we were worn out. My stomach growled. It had to be way past lunchtime by now.

We'd been having so much fun. We'd forgotten about food. But now we were starving!

We went back to the *Terra Grill* sign we'd hidden behind when we first landed. We figured we could eat at that restaurant.

Rudy told me that *terra* meant earth. Any kind of grill sounded good at this point. An Earth grill sounded even better!

We still hadn't seen the three old guys anywhere. So we figured we might as well eat.

Maybe the three old guys would be at the restaurant. They seemed to like restaurants.

On the outside, the Terra Grill looked like all the other sparkly lamp-shade buildings. But we were surprised when we walked inside.

It was completely dark. The only light came from a few flashlights and a big fire burning in the middle of the room. We looked up and saw stars overhead.

I recognized the Big Dipper, the Little Dipper, and Orion. They must have been fake Earth stars! They were just like the ones we saw at the planetarium.

They even had a fake Earth moon. Planet Zora didn't have a moon or any stars of its own as far as we'd seen.

The floor in the grill was dirt. It wasn't lit-up gold-dust dirt. It was real dirt—like on Earth.

The sign had said, "The most Earthlike place on Planet Zora." But this wasn't at all what we'd expected.

Several Zorians were sitting on huge logs. The logs were placed in a circle around a fire. It was just like a campfire on Earth.

This Zorian with a hunting cap on (earflaps and all) led us to a place on a log. Then he brought us sticks with hot dogs on them.

We had to stick them in the fire and cook our own. Everybody else was cooking their hot dogs too.

While we roasted our hot dogs, we tried to listen to the Zorians sitting around the fire. To our surprise, they were speaking Earth languages!

We heard English and Spanish. And I think I even heard some Japanese. Luckily, the earflap guy spoke in English.

I guess our disguises were working pretty well. No one was staring at us or anything.

When our hot dogs were almost done, this Zorian lady started throwing a fit. Her fingers were on fire. We could tell by all the fuss she was causing that this wasn't normal on Planet Zora.

Luckily, the earflap guy was standing nearby. He was holding a bucket of ketchup. He threw it on her hands without even thinking about it.

It was very messy. But the ketchup put out the flames quickly. Her fingers didn't even get burned.

It turned out that she was wearing some of those really long fake fingernails. You could buy them in drugstores on Earth.

I guess they were pretty flammable. Because she got her hot dog too close to the fire and POOF! Instant barbecued fingernails.

The earflap guy rushed her out of the

restaurant. She was fussing too much. It was ruining everyone else's good mood.

My hot dog looked really good. I was about to take my first bite when I felt a sharp sting. Ouch! Something had definitely bitten me.

Then Rudy slapped his arm. Something had bitten him too.

Soon all the Zorians were slapping at themselves too. But they were giggling about it.

Something was biting all of us. It was too dark. I couldn't see what it was.

Then Rudy whispered to me. I knew he was right—mosquitoes! We couldn't believe it.

We had no idea why they would have mosquitoes in a restaurant. But they sure did! And it was annoying!

Meanwhile, the smoke from the fire started blowing in our faces. We were coughing and slapping mosquitoes. At the same time, we were trying to eat our hot dogs.

All the Zorians seemed to be having fun. But not us. We would have left right then if we hadn't been so hungry.

Boy, were we glad we stayed! For dessert they brought out marshmallows. We roasted them on the same sticks we had used for the hot dogs.

A few mosquitoes got stuck on the marshmallows. But they still tasted good.

I cooked mine just right—burned on the outside, but gooey in the middle. Rudy just burned his to a crisp. Then he ate the whole thing in one bite. I don't think he even tasted the mosquitoes.

Then we got these tin mugs filled with coffee. Talk about bad! I don't like the taste of coffee all that much anyway. But I had made enough pots at the Galaxy Diner to know a bad cup when I tasted one. This was the worst ever!

I must have made a grossed-out face. The guy with the earflaps asked me what was wrong. He was about my age. And he was kind of cute in a Zorian kind of way.

I decided to help him out. I told him I could show him how to make a *real* cup of Earth coffee.

He looked thrilled. I was about to explain how to make the coffee when we heard a loud ROAR! I had seen and heard bears on TV. I knew that sound had to be a bear!

I also knew enough to be scared. We jumped up and ran out of there as fast as we could.

Rudy and I ran until we had to stop. We were gasping for breath and laughing so hard. Mosquitoes, smoke, and bears—what a crazy restaurant theme!

THE GALAXY DINER

Had the Zorians sat up there in their spaceships and watched people camping in the woods? We figured they must have seen a lot of campers! Did they think that was the way we ate every day?

We were still giggling when something tugged at my arm. I turned around. The earflap guy was standing there. He must have followed us.

He wanted to know what was so funny. Of course, we couldn't tell him. We didn't want to hurt his feelings.

He said his name was Lonzen. We thought he seemed nice. He still wanted me to show him how to make good coffee.

Lonzen told us they didn't have a real bear at the grill. It was just a tape recording. We felt better. So we all headed back to the Terra Grill.

Lonzen was grateful for the coffee lessons. He asked what he could do for us. I wanted to scream, "Take us to Earth!"

But of course, then he would know we were Earthlings. He might sell us to a science lab. They would might do horrible experiments on us.

So we just told him some of the truth. We told him that we were looking for our three friends. We described the three old guys—their purplish gray hair and striped shirts. We even told him about their screechy little laughs.

We said we really needed to find them. But we didn't say why. His eyes got really big and surprised-looking. He looked like he knew something about them.

I thought he wanted to tell us. But then he bit his tongue. He did suggest we check out some other Earth-theme restaurants.

Apparently, the Earth theme was really hot. Besides the Terra Grill, there was also the Seafood Supper Club, the Earth-a-teria, the Picnic Place, and the Luau Luncheonette. And those were just the restaurants nearby!

Lonzen gave us directions to the Seafood Supper Club. We wondered what we would see there!

6

The Seafood Supper Club

The first thing we noticed was the fog. It surrounded the Seafood Supper Club.

Then we noticed the smell. It reminded me of the time Uncle Roger took us to the Atlantic Ocean.

Sometimes there were dead fish lying on the burning sand. They had washed up with the tide. I always felt sorry for them.

That is, until I smelled that awful smell. The one you can always identify as dead fish.

Well, that was what it smelled like around the Seafood Supper Club. I was afraid to go inside. What if all the fish inside were dead?

I really liked live fish. They were fun to watch swimming around. But I wasn't fond of ones that had stopped swimming.

Rudy and I slowly pulled open the heavy wooden door to the restaurant. We were standing in a large, dark entryway.

The entryway was full of fog. It was thick and heavy. We could barely see anything. A foghorn sounded in the distance.

The dead-fish smell was heavier too. We couldn't escape it. Rudy wanted to leave. But I told him to wait just a minute.

Suddenly, a light splash of water slapped us in the face. It felt like ocean mist. A cool breeze blew through the room.

Then a hostess glided up to us. She was dressed like a mermaid. Long red hair flowed all the way down her back. I wondered if it was her real hair or a wig.

Her long skirt was covered with blue-green sequins that sparkled. It was so long that we couldn't see her feet at all.

She didn't speak to us. She just pinned fishing lures to our hats. Then she led us into the main dining room.

The dining room was beautiful. It wasn't dark or foggy or misty or smelly.

The color of the air was cool. It was a deep turquoise blue. Little shimmering lights glittered through it.

The air was damp against our skin. And it was so thick. We could almost touch it with our fingers.

The windows were portholes, like on a big ship. And every seat had a life preserver as a cushion.

The floor was covered with white sand mixed with silver glitter. Big purple and yellow sea fans waved gently as we walked by.

It felt like we were in a sunken ship on the bottom of the sea.

Then we realized that all the tables were full, but no one was eating. No one was making any noise either. It was quieter than a library.

We moved farther into the dining room. We had trouble following the hostess. Our legs didn't seem to be moving fast enough.

It was like we were walking underwater. We couldn't see or feel any water. And we weren't getting wet. But the air was as thick as water.

I thought I saw a bright blue fish swim by. Then a red one passed right in front of me. We realized there were fish swimming all around us.

Rudy decided to have some fun. He jumped up and did a flutter kick. It worked!

He went about three feet up and gently floated back down. I tried it too. Wow! We could swim in the blue air!

I leaped up and did a front flip. Soon Rudy and I were flipping back and forth. And no water was going up our noses!

The hostess must have realized we weren't following her anymore. I was right in the middle of an upside-down mermaid pose when she grabbed me. She roughly pulled Rudy and me forward.

Without a word, she led us to a table. She glared at us. Her eyes were colder than sharks' eyes. I'd hate to be a minnow around her at dinnertime.

We sat down and looked around. It seemed like even more fish were swimming by. But none of the Zorians were moving at all. No one came to take our orders either.

I leaned over and asked a Zorian what was up. He looked annoyed. He whispered for me to be quiet. He was afraid I would scare the fish away.

We sat there in silence for a few minutes. Then Rudy figured it out. The Zorians were waiting for their dinners as patiently as fishermen wait for fish on the side of a riverbank.

And they were waiting quietly. Everyone knew that fish were afraid of noise.

Patience and quiet were not my strong points. I looked around for the three old guys. I didn't see them anywhere. So I decided we should leave.

All of a sudden, fish hooks started dropping from the ceiling. Dozens of fish started swimming by. They came from every direction.

There were fish in every color and every size. There were schools of little yellow fish. And there were schools of big striped fish with bulging eyes and fat lips.

Two barracudas were chasing each other. Their sharp teeth glistened in the water. When I saw them, I decided to stay in my seat.

We heard a big splash. The Zorians started cheering and clapping.

The fish were so beautiful that we had forgotten about the fish hooks. But as they dropped closer to the table, we gasped. We couldn't believe what those hooks had caught.

There wasn't one fish! There was green seaweed and old shoes and rubber tires. A license plate from Michigan dropped in front of me. And a bunch of rusty tin cans fell in front of Rudy.

Was this dinner? We cracked up. Did Zorians think we ate *anything* that came from the sea?

Our laughter was bothering the others around us. They stared at us. We must have been disturbing their peaceful dinner.

We looked around one last time for the three old guys. There was no sign of them.

Then we spotted Lonzen near the door. He was talking seriously with another Zorian.

We tried to swim toward him. But I got tangled up in a fishing line. By the time Rudy got me untangled, Lonzen was gone.

The hostess looked mad at us again. I suppose we'd made a mess of the fishing line. But she gave us directions to the Earth-a-teria anyway.

We hurried out of the restaurant. On our way out, we tripped over a sea fan.

We glanced back to see if the hostess had noticed. But she was busy cuddling up to a barracuda.

7

The Earth-a-teria

We had a little trouble finding the Earth-a-teria. It was in an older section of Planet Zora. The lights all seemed a little dimmer here. The glittery gold dust had less sparkle.

Even the Zorians here didn't quite have the same shine as those in other areas. They moved a little slower too.

The theme behind the Earth-a-teria was an all-you-can-eat buffet. That seemed normal enough.

Before we went in, we watched a group of Zorians stumble out the door. Maybe I should say they *rolled* out the door. These guys were so full. They could barely stand up.

Their stomachs were huge! They were all holding their guts. Their faces looked dazed.

I tried to ask one about the three old guys. But he just stared blankly past me. Rudy and I shrugged our shoulders and went inside.

We couldn't believe the amount of food we saw there. Every Zorian had a plate with a huge pile of food. The air was thick with the smell of grease.

There was a long food bar. The Zorians were lined up along the buffet line. They were dishing out huge portions on their plates.

There was a large salad bar at one end. Piles of green lettuce overflowed from the bowl. Small bowls of salad toppings surrounded the lettuce-leaf mound.

The middle of the bar was stacked with lots of different dishes. I could see fried chicken, mashed potatoes, macaroni and cheese, and tacos. Rudy said the pizza looked good.

The desserts lay at the end of the long bar. We could see the Zorians loading their plates with cake, pie, and cookies. They even had an ice cream machine!

We looked around at the Zorians sitting at tables. We could tell which ones had just started eating. They were eating really fast.

One guy was eating so fast I swear we could see his stomach growing. I still feel full just thinking about it.

The ones who'd been there awhile were moving really slowly. They just stared straight ahead like they'd been hypnotized. They kept shoveling food into their mouths in slow motion.

Luckily, we were still full from the hot dogs and marshmallows. Because watching the Zorians stuff themselves wasn't very appetizing.

Unfortunately, we still didn't see the three old guys around anywhere. We turned to leave. Then we thought we saw Lonzen again. He was talking to a couple of Zorians near the exit.

We tried to get a better look. But some guy walked right in front of us. He had a huge mound of food on his plate. It was so huge that we couldn't see over it.

I admit I got a little impatient. I tried to get around him. BAM! I accidentally bumped his tray. I swear it was an accident.

His whole plate went flying. There was a loud crash and then . . . a big silence.

Food was everywhere. It was dripping off the chairs and walls. There were piles of mashed potatoes on the heads of some Zorians. Spaghetti noodles ran down the faces of innocent bystanders.

They sure were mad! And they were staring right at me! I didn't know whether to laugh or cry. So I just stood there. I was frozen like a zombie.

Thank goodness Rudy grabbed my hand and yanked me out of there. The Zorians tried to chase us. But they were so full they could hardly walk. They definitely couldn't run.

But we ran anyway—fast. Maybe faster than when we were racing. Luckily, we ran right into the Picnic Place.

8

The Picnic Place

We were getting a little tired of Planet Zora's crazy restaurants. But we really needed to find those three old guys so we could get home.

It wasn't that this was such a bad place or anything. But when you were scared you'd never get home, it made you want to get there that much worse.

Now, we loved to go on picnics. But after the restaurants we'd seen, we were a little hesitant to go inside the Picnic Place. We were pleasantly surprised!

It was beautiful. I have to hand it to the Zorians. They sure know how to make an indoor place look like an outdoor place.

On the outside, the Picnic Place was Zora's typical glittery lamp shade-shaped building. But inside, it was like we'd walked into the sunniest day on Earth.

There were rolling hills covered in flowers. The sun was shining brightly. We could even hear birds singing.

There were big maple trees everywhere. They were perfect for climbing. A red-and-white checked tablecloth rested under each tree.

Small groups of Zorians were sitting peacefully under the trees. They were eating from large picnic baskets.

Rudy and I raced to the nearest free tablecloth. It was under the biggest climbing tree there.

We looked in the picnic basket. We decided maybe we were hungry after all. There were peanut butter and jelly sandwiches, potato chips, and chocolate chip cookies. We also found a gallon of milk, some soda, and two big pieces of chocolate cake. Yum!

It was all delicious too. We were stuffed by the time we got to the chocolate cake. So we decided to save it for later.

We felt so warm and happy. We just lay back and looked at the sky. White puffy clouds in animal shapes floated by.

You know how people always thought they saw a bunny or a bear in the clouds? And you really had to use your imagination to see what they saw?

Sometimes you just pretended to see what they saw. But you really just saw another fluffy cloud. Or at most it looked like a giant cotton ball in the sky.

Well, at the Picnic Place, the clouds really *were* shaped like animals. The cutest were the sheep. But the dinosaurs were pretty cool too.

If we were going to be stuck on Planet Zora, this was sure a good place to be. I felt so good I forgot about finding the three old guys—at least for a moment.

The Zorians were flying kites all around us. Most of the kites were shaped like butterflies. They were every size and color you could imagine. I had never seen kites that beautiful on Earth.

The kites were flying right over our heads. They were so close. We felt the breeze from their wings. It was like we were in a giant butterfly world.

The kites seemed to crash a lot, though. So it was more like we were in the world of giant, clumsy butterflies.

There was this one huge butterfly kite. It was bigger than all the other kites. It was bigger than a car. For a kite, it was enormous!

I could tell Rudy really wanted to try flying it. So I went over and asked if he could have a turn. The Zorians were really nice. They offered to let us both fly kites.

Rudy flew the big butterfly kite. I flew a smaller one. Mine looked like a monarch butterfly.

Rudy made the big kite dive low and climb fast. It even turned somersaults. The Zorians were amazed.

Every time our kites would come close to crashing or getting caught in a tree, the Zorians would cheer. When the kites started going back up, they would screech with laughter. We finally figured out that they wanted us to crash the kites!

The Zorians must have seen a lot of kites crashing on Earth. Usually people laughed when that happened. Now the Zorians thought that crashing was the fun part of flying kites.

No wonder all those butterflies kept smashing into the ground. The Zorians kept running back and forth *trying* to tangle their strings up.

When their kites came close to the ground, they would let out all their string really fast. That would send their kites crashing to the ground.

Crashing kites is almost harder than keeping them up in the air. You have to keep getting them back up in order to crash them again. It was a challenging way to fly to kites.

Rudy had been flying the big butterfly for about ten minutes. Suddenly, he crashed it right into our tree. It got tangled in the highest branches.

I thought the Zorians might get mad since it was their best kite. But they just cheered and slapped Rudy on the back.

All that crashing tired us out. We went back to our tree and lay on the tablecloth to rest. I lay there looking up through the branches at the tangled kite. I thought about how great life was.

Suddenly, Rudy started tickling my leg. At least I thought it was Rudy. I kept telling him to stop.

He kept saying, "Stop what?"

Then I felt a sharp pinch. "Hey!" I screamed. But Rudy wasn't even near me.

I looked down. I was covered in ants—big red ants! They were the biggest red ants I'd ever seen.

They must have come for the chocolate cake and found me instead.

I started screaming. Rudy tried to help me. We frantically brushed at the ants.

All of a sudden, Rudy cried out. He was covered with ants too.

I felt another hard pinch. OUCH! We were both crying and yelling. Then we started to panic.

A loud crack boomed in the sky. It was thunder. The sky got dark and there was a huge flash of lightning. Rain started pouring down.

We ran out into the rain to wash the ants off. All the Zorians came running. They wanted to see what all the yelling was about.

It was raining really hard now. The ants just slid right off us. They were all gone as quickly as they'd come.

I was just about to breathe a sigh of relief when I noticed Rudy looking panicked. I looked down and understood why.

All of our gold glitter dust had washed off. We tried to run back under the tree. But it was too late. Our disguises were ruined.

The Zorians crowded around us. They stared at our pale skin. Then one shouted out, "Earthlings!"

They all started racing towards us. We jumped in the tree and started climbing up as fast as we could.

The Zorians climbed up after us. We climbed higher and higher. But the Zorians kept coming.

Rudy climbed right up to the big butterfly kite. He started untangling it. I knew what he was up to. I was right behind him, screaming for him to hurry.

The closest Zorian grabbed my foot. Just then, Rudy got the kite untangled. The huge kite took off.

We both grabbed the heavy kite string. We held on for dear life. I yanked my foot away from the Zorian. We were free!

The wind and rain were blowing hard now. The kite started doing somersaults near the tree. We hung on with all our might.

The Zorians were just waiting for us to crash. Then they could get us. The kite started swooping down. It headed straight toward the top tree branches.

Right before we hit, we felt a hard tug on the kite string. I thought sure they'd gotten us. But instead of crashing, we went soaring away.

We flew above all the treetops. We soared right through the sheep-shaped clouds. That butterfly kite flew us straight to the exit of the Picnic Place.

The Picnic Place

We landed on the ground with a thud. We saw Lonzen holding the other end of our kite string.

Lonzen had rescued us! He threw us a note written on a paper airplane. Then he yelled for us to run. We ran like the wind.

9

The Luau Luncheonette

We ran for at least ten minutes. Then we stopped to read Lonzen's message. These words were written on the paper airplane.

The three old guys
will be performing at the
Luau Luncheonette
in 35 minutes.

He'd written the directions down too. We couldn't imagine what those three old guys would be performing. But we weren't about to miss it. We were really ready to get off this planet!

Even without Lonzen's directions, it wouldn't have been hard to find the Luau Luncheonette. Hundreds of Zorians were lined up outside. We couldn't have missed it.

Those in line were waiting to get in. It was a two-hour wait. And, by now, the three old guys would be performing in 15 minutes.

We had to get in there. But we didn't know how to get past the crowd.

After being chased by the mob at Picnic Place, we didn't think it was a good idea to cut in line. Besides that, we didn't have time to redo our disguises. We still had our hats on. But if anybody really looked at us, we'd be discovered in a minute.

We were trying to stay hidden. So we darted around to the back of the building. We didn't see any back doors or windows to sneak through. It looked hopeless.

Suddenly, Rudy saw a round button with extra sparkle. It was on the outside wall. He was about to push it when a hidden panel slid open right beside us.

Three Zorian hula dancers in real grass skirts walked out. They almost bumped into us.

Rudy tipped his cowboy hat low over his eyes. "Pardon me, ladies," he said in a low cowboy drawl.

The hula dancers started giggling. They forgot to close the panel behind them. We slipped inside.

It turned out that the secret panel was an entrance to a backstage dressing room. The room was full of Zorian hula dancers in grass skirts. They were wearing leis around their necks. Some of the dancers were putting on makeup in front of mirrors.

The Luau Luncheonette

Rudy nudged me and pointed to a dressing table. There were three wig stands. Two were empty. But one had a gray wig with a purplish glow to it.

We'd know that hair anywhere! It had to belong to one of the three old guys. We'd never considered that the funny hair might be wigs!

A luau with hula dancers made perfect sense. But we wondered what the three old guys had to do with it.

A tall, broad man turned around and saw us. He was wearing a flashy shirt with palm trees on it. He looked like he was in charge.

He started yelling at us to hurry. He threw us two grass skirts. We had no choice but to put them on!

The hula dancers started rushing past us. The guy in charge pushed us out the door with them. He shoved us right onto the stage!

The crowd was roaring. The place was packed. A drummer started playing. And the dancers started doing the hula.

Rudy and I started swaying along with them. We tried to copy their moves. I was sure glad Uncle Roger hadn't let me quit taking ballet lessons.

I hoped I was doing better than Rudy. He looked hopeless. After he tripped over his grass skirt twice, I couldn't watch him anymore. It was too painful.

I tried to look for the three old guys in the crowd. But the lights were shining right in my eyes. I couldn't see a thing.

Rudy finally got smart. He hid behind a cardboard palm tree so he wouldn't have to dance anymore.

It was a good thing he did. He was starting to attract some attention. And attention was one thing we didn't want!

Finally, the music stopped. The hula dancers took a bow as the crowd clapped and cheered. I bowed right along and almost followed them off the stage. Then the cardboard palm tree coughed loudly.

I jumped behind the palm tree with Rudy. We looked around the restaurant.

A long, skinny table ran along the back wall. It was covered with a tablecloth. It had bright purple and orange flowers on it.

The table was loaded with delicious luau treats. There were lots of meat dishes—fish and pork and chicken.

The center of the table held mounds of colorful, fresh fruits. The pineapples, guavas, apples, bananas, and papayas all looked sweet and refreshing.

For dessert, there were macadamia nuts and coconut pudding. We wished we had time to eat!

Suddenly, Rudy pointed in the direction of the opposite stage door. He had spotted the three old guys! They were walking onto the stage.

The three old guys were dressed in their usual striped shirts and gray wigs. One was carrying a long bamboo pole. He tossed one end of the pole to the second old guy.

The music began playing again. The third old guy started doing the limbo!

We had done the limbo once in gym class. We had to bend backwards and try to get under the pole. But we couldn't touch the pole or knock it down.

Ms. Johnson, our teacher, lowered the pole every time we went under. It got harder and harder. Finally, we ended up walking like crabs, almost flat on our backs. The kids with the shortest legs had it easy.

It was fun at first. But then some of the boys thought it was more fun to knock the pole down on purpose. Ms. Johnson got really mad. She made us all run laps instead.

Anyway, the three old guys were making a big joke out of it. They were acting like clowns trying to do the limbo. Maybe they were making fun of Earthlings for being so silly.

The old guy going under the pole knocked it off every time. He acted really disappointed. Everybody in the crowd burst out laughing.

Then the pole knocked off the old guy's hair. We watched the wig go flying. We looked back at the old guy—only it wasn't an old guy. It was Lonzen!

We couldn't believe it! We bet the other two "old" guys were just kids too. They were all just pretending to be old.

No wonder they always wore striped shirts. Those were their Earthling costumes. The wigs helped disguise their real ages.

We couldn't wait to talk to Lonzen. But he was busy pulling Zorians from the audience up on stage. The audience members joined the limbo contest.

There were about 20 Zorians lined up to get under the pole. Everyone was having a ball. The music was playing. The crowd was dancing and laughing.

Now I knew why this was such a popular place. It was really fun.

Rudy and I got caught up in the excitement. We started dancing and goofing around behind the cardboard palm tree. It was very noisy. We didn't have to worry about being quiet here.

Then I started hula dancing with a little too much energy. My Uncle Roger would have said I was "getting carried away."

Well, that was probably true. But it was hard to dance the hula with your arms stuck straight by your sides. So I swung my arms out just as I was doing a really fast ballet turn and . . . BOOM! I hit the cardboard palm tree so hard it went crashing down.

The tree fell right in the middle of the limbo line. It barely missed several dancing Zorians.

Rudy and I just stood there. We were frozen in place. We certainly got the attention we didn't want.

The crowd grew quiet. Everyone stared at us. My face turned cherry red with embarrassment. And I started to feel scared too.

Rudy nudged me and we ran toward the stage exit. I yelled out, "I'm sorry!"

I meant it too. We heard the crowd running and yelling. Doors slammed behind us. We thought we were going superfast. But Lonzen ran right past us.

He led us down a long, dark hallway. We kept running after him. Just when I didn't think I could run another step, we came to a steep staircase. It was not like any staircase I'd ever seen before.

10

The Escape

The staircase was really skinny. There was just enough room for one kid to go up at a time. No adults would fit. It was too narrow.

There were walls on both sides of the staircase. There wasn't even enough room for railings. No one who'd ever eaten at the Earth-a-teria would ever fit.

The Escape

There was also a thin fog rising from the steps. It was the kind of smoky fog used in magic shows.

The walls were made of the same lit-up sparkly metal as everything else on Planet Zora. But the steps were different.

The steps were made of lit-up metal too—but not just gold glittery metal. The steps had millions of colors in them.

The little glittery lights flashed and sparkled in every color I could ever imagine. They were really pretty.

We started climbing the sparkly staircase. Lonzen warned us not to touch the steps with our hands. He didn't explain why.

We heard the footsteps of the Zorians who were chasing us. They were getting farther away. I wanted to slow down. But we kept moving.

I was having a hard time keeping up with Lonzen. He was flying up those stairs like he'd done it a million times. Finally, I just had to rest.

Between all the running and hula dancing, my legs were killing me. I stopped to sit down. I told Rudy I'd catch up in a minute. What a mistake!

When I sat down, I was shocked by how cold the step was. I forgot about Lonzen's warning. I rested my hands beside me on the step. My hands stuck to the steps!

Have you ever put your tongue on an ice cube? When you try to pull it off, your tongue sticks. Sometimes there's even a burning sensation. Usually you have to wait until the ice melts before your tongue can pull away.

Well, that's what this was like. My hands were burning and I couldn't move them. When I tried, it hurt worse.

And these steps weren't going to melt! I was really stuck.

I called out for Rudy and Lonzen to come back and help me. They returned quickly. But when Lonzen saw my stuck hands, he was horrified.

He explained that his spaceship was scheduled to leave in five minutes. There was no way to delay takeoff.

Lonzen felt awful about it. But he didn't think there was any way to get me unstuck. He had no choice but to leave me behind.

I looked at Rudy and told him to go on without me. I didn't really want him to go. But there was no sense in both of us getting stuck on Planet Zora.

But Rudy did some fast thinking. I already told you he was smart. Well, this proved it.

He bent his head down to one of my hands. Then he started blowing really hard. His breath was hot from running up all those stairs.

At first, nothing happened. But he kept blowing harder and harder.

Suddenly the steps' colored lights dimmed a little. My hands broke loose. I was free! I gave Rudy the biggest hug.

We all raced up the stairs. I was so happy to be unstuck. I didn't even feel how tired my legs were. We ran all the way to the top.

Lonzen pushed open the heavy metal door at the top of the stairs. The outside air cooled our flushed faces. We were standing on top of the Luau Luncheonette.

The spaceship was right in front of us. Its lights were flashing like crazy. The engine was making that high-pitched whistling sound again. The entry panel was open.

We all ran and jumped in. The other two guys were already inside. Lonzen told us where to sit. He even made us buckle up.

Lonzen told us it would be much nicer riding in seats. This time we wouldn't be crammed in the entryway like we were on the ride *to* Planet Zora.

We felt the spaceship start shaking and spinning like before. We grabbed our seats as the ship lifted off. We were on our way home.

11

The Truth Comes Out

I must have fallen asleep. The next thing I
knew, I felt a big bump. We had landed.

I looked out the window. We were surrounded
by trees. Their leaves fluttered in the crisp air. I
never thought I'd be so happy to be smack-dab in
the middle of the scary woods.

The Truth Comes Out

Before we got out of the spaceship, we wanted some answers. Lonzen was happy to answer our questions.

It turned out the other two "old" guys were just kids too. One was named Rikizon. The other was named Zenbob.

We asked why they had waited so long to tell us they were the three old guys. They said they had to be sure they could trust us first. They didn't want us to tell anybody else on Planet Zora how often they came to Earth.

Even though Zorians traveled a lot, the head Zorians discouraged travelers from going to one place too many times. They didn't want any Zorians to be discovered.

Lonzen, Rikizon, and Zenbob loved it on Earth. That was why they came almost every night. But they didn't want to get caught. Then they'd have to stop coming.

They left Planet Zora right after their show at the Luau Luncheonette. It was easy since they were already wearing their Earth disguises. They didn't come to the Galaxy Diner on Mondays because there was no show on Sunday nights.

The three guys asked us some questions as well. They wanted to know why we'd followed them to their spaceship. They were worried that we had suspected they weren't Earthlings.

We assured them we had never even considered that. We had thought there was something odd about them. But we'd never thought they were from another planet. We'd followed them and gotten into all that trouble out of pure boredom.

We told them we'd never been anywhere except Earth and Planet Zora. They didn't believe it.

They wanted to make a deal with us. If we would be their Earth tour guides, they would take us to other planets someday.

Rudy and I agreed quickly. We were excited about getting to visit other planets. We also thought it would be fun to show Zorians around Earth. I planned my first tour-guide duty. I'd be buying new wigs that didn't leave any purple stains!

We had to promise to never tell anybody about Planet Zora. And we had to keep the three old guys' real identities a secret. We couldn't act any differently when they came in for breakfast at the Galaxy Diner.

We worked out a secret-message system. To leave messages for each other, we would write notes on Galaxy Diner napkins. Then we would put them under the sugar in the sugar bowl.

But we'd leave just a corner of the napkin sticking out. That way we could spot the messages without having to dig through the sugar. Uncle Roger would appreciate that!

It sounded like a pretty good deal to us. We gave them our promise right away. We thanked them for bringing us home.

Waving good-bye, we jumped down onto the grassy clearing. We glanced back at the spaceship. We wanted one last look.

Then we headed straight for the Galaxy Diner.

12

Home at Last

The Galaxy Diner had never looked so good! I was so happy to be home—on Earth.

It was getting dark out now. The dinner crowd was just arriving.

Through the window, we saw Uncle Roger talking to some customers. We had no idea what day it was. We hoped he hadn't been too worried about us. We were sure we were in big trouble.

Rudy and I tried to make up a realistic story to explain our disappearance. But nothing we came up with sounded quite right. Finally, we gave up. We decided to take our chances with Uncle Roger.

But when we walked inside, Uncle Roger barely paid us any attention. He hardly noticed us at all.

But Quasar sure did. She ran over to greet us and rub against our legs.

But when she got next to us, she stopped suddenly. Her fur stood on end. She let out a loud whine.

Quasar knew right away where we'd been— and she wasn't happy about it. We had to rub her ears for five minutes before she forgave us.

Then we approached Uncle Roger. He laughed and asked us what on Earth we'd been up to.

We answered honestly, "Nothing on Earth."

I asked Uncle Roger what day it was. He looked at me like I was being silly. He said it was still Saturday as far as he knew.

Then he looked at me like he was waiting for something. He thought I was telling him a joke. He was waiting for the punch line.

Of course, I didn't have one since I wasn't joking. But then Rudy thought of one quickly. He said it wasn't any day. It was night!

Uncle Roger laughed, even though it wasn't very funny. Then he told us to go home before it got too dark.

I couldn't believe it was still Saturday! That meant we'd done all that running around in one day. No wonder I was so tired.

13

Lunch As Usual

So that was what happened after work last Saturday. I don't care whether you believe me or not. Just as long as you keep it to yourself.

We had a pretty big lunch crowd today. The fair finally left town. People are ready for some real food again. I'm back handing out menus and refilling coffee cups.

THE GALAXY DINER

Lonzen, Rikizon, and Zenbob came in earlier. They acted totally normal. I almost thought I'd imagined our whole adventure.

Then Rudy pointed to my feet. My shoes were still leaving glittery gold footprints wherever I walked. Rudy keeps sweeping them up behind me.

The three guys are sitting in the corner booth laughing at some alien story in the paper as usual. They're acting like nothing ever happened.

I wonder if they'll leave me a secret message. In a way, I hope they don't—at least not for a while. I want to hang around the Galaxy Diner for a while before I go on any more adventures.

There's a group of tourists I've never seen before sitting at the front table. I can hear them talking about the Galaxy Diner. They're saying that eating in a flying saucer is a really crazy restaurant theme.

I sure could tell them some stories about crazy restaurant themes. But instead I'll just go over there and ask them if they want to try a Milky Way milk shake.